BATMAN & ROBIN ADVENTURES

DC COMICS SUPER HEROES

THE JOKER'S MAGIC MAYHEM

BY J. E. BRIGHT

ILLUSTRATED BY
LUCIANO VECCHIO

BATMAN CREATED BY BOB KANE

CONTENTS

CHAPTER 1

MAGIC AND MAYHEM

"Santoro is a master of mesmerism," said Tim Drake as he followed Bruce Wayne down the aisle of the newly renovated Monarch Theatre. "He can hypnotize and control anyone. He does all the classic tricks, too."

For once, Tim – the secret identity of crime fighter Robin – wasn't talking about a super-villain's nefarious powers. He and Bruce were attending a charity performance by the Magnificent Santoro. The world-famous magician was part of the celebration for the grand re-opening of the theatre.

Bruce shook hands with local celebrities and business people he knew as they moved towards their seats. The elite of Gotham City would be surprised if they knew that he was actually Batman! They only knew Bruce as the billionaire benefactor, who had given nearly a million dollars to the Monarch's renovation.

"Beautiful work fixing this theatre," Mayor Grange told Bruce as they passed by her. "It's truly a fitting memorial to your parents now."

"Thank you, Mayor," replied Bruce. "It was unfortunate that it had fallen into disrepair."

"Fixing the theatre benefits the whole neighbourhood," added Tim.

Bruce's parents had been murdered when he was a little boy, right outside this theatre. The traumatic event had led Bruce to swear revenge on all criminals and ultimately become Batman.

"Enjoy the show," Mayor Grange said, and she sat down after Bruce and Tim shuffled past her.

"And we couldn't let this location be a hideout for criminals anymore," Tim whispered to Bruce as they sat down in the front row. "Imagine the Joker's nerve setting up his headquarters in here for a while."

"If there's anything the Joker has," replied Bruce, "it's nerve."

They both fell silent as the lights dimmed. The audience settled down behind them, and everyone applauded as the curtains opened.

A young woman in a sparkly silver gown pushed a tall, fancy cabinet onto the stage. She smiled as she opened the wooden cabinet, showing that it was empty inside. Then she shut the door and began to spin the whole cabinet, faster and faster.

The woman hopped up on the foot of the cabinet and twirled with it, her dress glittering as the box spun to a blur. Then she put down her foot. **STOMP!** The cabinet stopped abruptly. The door swung open with an outpouring of dry ice vapour, and out stepped the Magnificent Santoro.

The audience applauded as the thin man in a tuxedo took a deep bow. He wore a tall turban with a spinning emerald embedded in a hollow in front. The turban stayed perched on his head even during the deepest part of his bow. He swirled his long, red cape behind him as he strode to the front of the stage.

"Nice entrance," whispered Tim.

Bruce nodded. "Impressive trick, too," he said. "It must be much more difficult to get in and out of that cabinet when it's twirling like that."

"Welcome!" announced Santoro as the applause subsided. "I see you've met Rachelle, my assistant. Take a bow, my dear."

Rachelle curtsied and smiled.

"And now, lovely Rachelle, exit stage left," continued Santoro.

With a kick, Rachelle pushed the open cabinet towards the left side of the stage. She ran faster, shoving the open box ahead of her. Then she jumped in and shut the door.

The cabinet slowed to a stop against the left side curtain. Then the door swung open.

Rachelle was gone.

After Rachelle's disappearance, Santoro pulled everyone's focus by performing a simple trick with cups and small green balls on a floating table.

"A simple misdirection trick," whispered Tim. "But he used an amazing number of combinations with just three cups."

Following the cup and balls trick, Santoro raised his arms. The lights darkened to a spooky purple. Wisps of dry ice vapour wafted around him. The emerald spinning in the front of his turban glowed an eerie green.

"There is a mysterious power that links all things," Santoro intoned in a calm voice. "It is an invisible plasma, connecting both inanimate objects and creatures endowed with life. If one controls this harmonic energy, one may control any mind with mental magnetism. This is how I mesmerize."

Bruce glanced over his shoulder at the audience. Most people were staring at Santoro on stage, their mouths open in amazement, as though already hypnotized.

Bruce let out a low chuckle ... until he looked over at Tim to share the joke. He saw that his ward was as slack-jawed as everyone else. Santoro was certainly a terrific showman!

"Young man, please join me up here on stage," Santoro said, and he gestured towards the audience.

A clean-cut teenage boy stood from his aisle seat and strode to the stage, hurrying up the stairs on the side.

"And madam?" asked Santoro, beckoning again. "If you would join me as well."

An elegant older woman leaned on her husband's shoulder as she slid past him into the aisle. She held up the side hem of her gown as she walked up to stand beside the teenager.

Santoro fixed them both with an intense stare. Wild music swelled from backstage, and the vapour thickened as the emerald in Santoro's turban flashed more quickly.

"Good people," said Santoro, his voice echoing through the hall, "listen to the soft hum that connects all things in our universe. Focus on that murmur of power, and feel it harmonizing with you, with every cell in your body, with every thought in your mind."

Bruce felt unnerved by how quiet the audience had become. Nobody was shuffling or coughing or whispering. They were all lost in total concentration. On stage, the teenager and the woman had matching blank expressions as they swayed on their feet.

"Now, young man and lovely lady," said Santoro. "You believe you are chickens."

Instantly, the teenager dropped into an awkward squat, shuffling his feet and bobbing his head.

The woman leaned over beside him, waggling her bent arms like wings. She let out a series of clucks.

The teen boy threw his head back and crowed like a rooster.

"Now, wake!" Santoro commanded. He clapped his hands.

Both the teenager and the woman froze in place. Sheepish smiles crossed their faces as they stood up.

The audience exploded in applause, hoots and laughter.

"Thank you very much," Santoro told his assistants. "You've been wonderful. Please, take your seats."

The crowd cheered for the lady and the teenager as they made their way back down, both with wide grins on their faces.

"That hat could be dangerous in the wrong hands," said Tim.

Bruce shook his head. "Mesmerism is a trick. It's only an illusion."

"I don't know," replied Tim. "I felt really relaxed and willing to follow his suggestions."

"Don't let anyone ever get in your head," Bruce warned. "Always stay in control."

"Ladies and gentlemen!" Santoro called out. "The next illusion I will perform for you tonight is my most dangerous. If I do it correctly, you may consider it my signature Santoro trick, for which I am justly famous. If I fail, we all must fear for our lives."

Santoro raised his hand, and a long, rectangular, silver curtain lowered from above the stage until it reached the floorboards. Lights flashed, shimmering off the shiny satin curtain. *MOOO!* A loud animal bellow rumbled throughout the theatre, vibrating in the audience's chests.

"Ladies and gentlemen," intoned Santoro, "I give you ... the vanishing bull!"

The curtain dropped, tumbling onto the stage. Behind it was a gigantic steel cage, and inside, spot-lit with red lights, was an enormous bull with gleaming horns. The bull shook his head and pawed the ground with his hoof, snorting in fury.

The audience gasped as the bull rammed into the side of the cage with his shoulder. *SCREECH!* The whole steel frame slid sideways, grinding against the stage.

A few shrieks came from the audience, along with nervous murmurs.

"Wait!" shouted Santoro. "Do not panic!" He bravely faced the enraged bull, with the emerald in his turban spinning wildly. "He, too, may hear the power of attraction that connects all things. Shhhh, and let us all open ourselves to wonder. Let us all listen."

After a moment of deep silence in the theatre, the bull lowered its head. Its gaze softened. Santoro raised his hands, and the bull relaxed in his cage.

The audience began to applaud.

BANG!

With a surprising bright flash, an explosion burst on stage right. Clouds of stinky green smoke billowed up. Santoro stumbled backwards, and the crowd screamed.

As the smoke cleared, a man could be seen standing where the explosion occurred. A spotlight shone down on him. He had bright green hair, a pale white face and a crazy gleam in his eyes.

"Oof," said the Joker, fanning the fumes with his hand. "I guess I used too much gunpowder."

Bruce jumped to his feet. "Someone call 911!"

"On it," said Tim, turning on his mobile phone and punching in the numbers.

The Joker grinned at Bruce. "Oh, sit down, Wayne," he sneered. "You're the most boring billionaire ever."

"Get off my stage this instant," Santoro told the Joker imperiously, "before I make you disappear."

"Ha-ha," said the Joker. "Watch what I can make disappear." He grabbed the corner of the satin curtain. *SWISH!* With a flourish, the Joker swooped it over the bull's cage.

When the sheet dropped, the steel bars of the cage had vanished, as though they had never existed. The bull turned his head to the audience and mooed, uncertain what to do with his new freedom.

GASP! The entire audience inhaled sharply in unison.

"Ole!" the Joker shouted, posing like a matador and clapping his hands loudly.

The bull's eyes widened in surprise and then narrowed in anger. *PFFT! PFFT!* He snorted out of his flaring nostrils.

The massive muscular steer charged straight at Santoro.

CHAPTER 2
ANIMAL CONTROL

"Mad bull!" screamed the magician. Santoro turned and ran, his long red cape flapping. He fell once onto his knees, and his turban flopped off onto the stage. Then he jumped to his feet and leaped into the audience, right as the bull barrelled into the space where he had been.

Bruce and Tim ducked as the magician crashed into the people behind them, tangling his limbs with theirs. He scrambled free and crawled over people's laps into the main aisle, where he raced towards the exit.

To avoid stepping on anyone, Bruce pushed himself up onto the top of the back of his seat. He raced along the headrests, with Tim right behind him.

The bull hopped off the edge of the stage and landed in the aisle. **MOOO!** He bellowed loudly and charged after Santoro.

"Everyone stay in your seats!" shouted Bruce. He firmly pushed an older gentleman down into his plush seat, preventing him from entering the aisle.

"Please do not panic!" added Tim. "The police will be here in minutes!"

Bruce frowned as he noticed two men by the exit door. Both were wearing baggy jumpsuits and clown masks. The goons held baseball bats. "The Joker's not alone," he hissed to Tim. "We need to help Santoro. Then we'll return and deal with the Joker."

"Follow that bull," said Tim.

They raced up the aisle together, catching up close behind the charging bull. The masked henchmen opened the exit doors, allowing Santoro to scamper outside.

"Don't let Wayne out!" the Joker screamed from the stage.

But as the bull raced through the exit doors after Santoro, Bruce and Tim were so close behind the enraged animal that the Joker's goons couldn't get close enough to stop them. They swung their baseball bats, but Bruce ducked under one, and Tim sidestepped the other's swing.

Outside, the twilight evening was lit by streetlamps. The busy street instantly became mayhem from the bull chasing Santoro. Passersby screamed and scrambled away. Cars skidded as drivers pulled up short.

The theatre's exit doors slammed and locked behind Bruce and Tim.

The bull cornered Santoro between a magazine stand and a crumpled taxi that had struck a lamppost.

"Tim, distract that bull," Bruce ordered.

Tim instantly ran up alongside the bull, yelling to pull its attention away from Santoro. The bull tilted his horn towards Tim, warning him not to get closer.

Bruce spotted a large delivery truck halfway down the block. The truck's rolling back door was open, and a long ramp reached down to the street. The truck was partially full with cardboard boxes.

"Santoro!" yelled Bruce. "Run towards that truck! Full speed!" Then he led the way, with Santoro following close behind.

Tim waved his arms, trying to get the bull's attention, but the bull ignored him and raced after Santoro's flapping cape.

AAAHHHH! Santoro screamed as he ran faster.

Bruce reached the truck a few seconds ahead of Santoro. He peered at the labels on the few boxes inside. They contained soft grocery items like paper towels, nothing that was too expensive and nothing that would harm the bull.

"Wait," Bruce told Santoro, gripping him by the shoulders. *SWISH!* He ripped the cape off the magician, then shoved Santoro to the side. Holding the red cape, Bruce flicked it with a flourish in front of the truck's open compartment.

The bull galloped at the fluttering cape.

Bruce let go of the cape as the bull barrelled into it.

Blinded by the cape in his face, the bull continued into the truck, colliding with cardboard packages. **CRUNCH!**

CLUNK! Bruce pulled the door down, trapping the bull inside.

The bull shifted around inside, wobbling the whole truck back and forth, but it couldn't escape.

"Good work, Bruce," said Tim.

Sirens shrieked from down the street, and Bruce could see both an ambulance and a police car heading their way.

Bruce kneeled beside Santoro. "We have to run now," he told the magician. "But help is on its way. Tell the police to call animal control before opening that truck."

"I will," replied Santoro, gasping for breath. "Thank you!"

Bruce and Tim dashed down the street, pushing past onlookers, slowing down so they blended into the city crowd.

"We have a hidden equipment cache not far from here," said Bruce.

"I know the one," replied Tim, running beside him. "I checked it recently. It has everything we need."

They found a narrow alley. Deep in its murky shadows, they pushed aside a heavy rubbish skip. Behind it was a compartment hidden by a false front of fake bricks. Inside that was a pair of uniforms, backup Utility Belts and weapons.

Shielded by the skip, Bruce and Tim changed into Batman and Robin.

"Let's go and rescue that audience," growled Batman.

They climbed up a fire escape ladder in the back of the alley and emerged on a moonlit rooftop overlooking Gotham City. From there, it took less than five minutes to run, jump and swing across the buildings back towards the Monarch Theatre.

On top of the Monarch, Robin pried open an exit door on the roof. Batman pressed a finger to his lips as they stepped downstairs, warning Robin to stay silent.

The third floor's offices and dressing rooms were all empty. The Joker's henchmen had probably forced everyone down to the theatre's ground floor. But as Batman had suspected, one lone henchman in a clown mask stood guard on the stairwell landing between the second and third floors.

Responding to Batman's hand signal, Robin attracted the goon's attention. As the henchman stepped up into the hall, holding his baseball bat, Batman dropped down behind him. *POW!* With a quick punch he knocked the goon unconscious.

After locking the henchman in a supply cupboard, Batman and Robin hurried down a floor. They surprised another goon coming out of a women's bathroom. They each grabbed one of her arms and tightened plastic restraints on her wrists and ankles. Then they stuffed her back in the bathroom.

Batman led Robin along a short corridor past the bathrooms and found the door to the upper lighting rig above the stage. They tiptoed inside, closed the door behind them, and silently stepped out onto the catwalk over the backstage area.

Now they could hear the Joker onstage, talking to the captive audience.

"Think about the hate that connects all things in the universe," the Joker intoned. "In the chaos of existence there is madness we all share. Is hate too strong a word for you? It's not too strong for me, but so I don't offend you, how about I say *irritation* instead? Think about the annoyance that binds all people together. There is so much *bother* in the universe. Relax into the magical misery and mayhem that is the sticky stuff of existence."

"What's he doing?" whispered Robin.

"I believe he is trying to hypnotize them," replied Batman. "In his own insane way."

"I feel sick just listening to him," said Robin.

"Block him out as much as possible," said Batman. "We need to stop him quickly. He cannot be allowed to terrorize this theatre and disgrace my parents' memory any more than he has already."

They stepped quietly along the catwalk, crossing over the dark area behind the curtains. Down below, they could see Santoro's sets and tricks lined up, waiting to be wheeled onstage when the magician needed them. Batman recognized the vanishing cabinet from the opening act near the curtain.

On the far right, Batman could see a goon in the lighting and sound booth, working the controls. He and Robin ducked down to avoid getting spotted by him, but luckily the henchman was concentrating on what was going on onstage.

Inching along the catwalk, Batman and Robin moved away from the booth, past the side lighting rigs that shielded them from the henchman's view. From there, they could peer around the left curtain onto the stage.

The Joker stood at the front and centre of the stage, chattering to the audience.

Two henchmen patrolled the aisles in their clown masks.

The crowd remained seated, staring up at the Joker. They had the same blank expression on their faces as when Santoro had hypnotized them, but instead of looking amazed and delighted, they all looked absolutely horrified.

The Joker was wearing Santoro's tall turban with the spinning emerald in front. He had a long sword scabbard dangling from his hip.

Sidestepping a bit more, Batman peered deeper on the stage. Behind the Joker was a tall transparent box of thick bulletproof glass in a steel frame. On top of this case was a gigantic tank of water. The whole contraption looked like an enormous water cooler in an office. Trapped inside the bottom box, banging her fists uselessly against the inside of the glass, was Mayor Marion Grange.

"What's he doing to the mayor?" asked Robin.

Batman shook his head. "He's taken her hostage," he replied grimly. "That looks like the equipment for a famous trick, invented by the greatest escape artist of all time, Harry Houdini. It's called the Water Torture Cell. If the Joker releases that water into the cell, the mayor won't know how to escape. She'll drown in minutes."

"So how do we stop the Joker while he has Mayor Grange held hostage?" whispered Robin.

"We use a few tricks of our own," said Batman. "And we get her out of there."

The lights wobbled around the Joker until he was eerily glowing in a triple spotlight.

"Now are you all deeply hypnotized or whatever, folks?" the Joker asked the audience. "Oh, fantastic! I think you are!" Out of the long scabbard on his hip, he pulled out a wickedly sharp, skinny sword. Its narrow length gleamed sharply in the lights. "So who wants to volunteer for some sword swallowing?"

CHAPTER 3

HOCUS POCUS

"That's it," said Batman. "The Joker's not playing around anymore. He's definitely going to hurt someone. We need to stop him right now."

"But how?" asked Robin. "He has the mayor in a tank that could drown her. He has the whole crowd vulnerable to him and his henchmen. I don't even want to know what they would do with those baseball bats."

Batman peered around the audience again. He scowled as two of the Joker's goons pulled a beautiful woman to her feet.

"Batman, isn't that Julie?" Robin hissed.

"I see her," replied Batman. It was Julie Madison, who he used to date as Bruce Wayne, until she married a rich European prince. He hadn't known she was even in Gotham City.

The henchmen shoved her towards the stage where the Joker waited with his sharp sword.

"But there is someone else I *can't* see," Batman continued. "Rachelle, Santoro's assistant. She's not in the audience, so she must be hiding somewhere backstage. Find her, Robin, while I stop the Joker from hurting Julie."

"Of course," said Robin. "Rachelle can help us turn Santoro's tricks against the Joker. I'll find her."

He hoisted himself over the guardrail of the catwalk, then jumped to a cable dangling from the ceiling to the floor. Robin slid down the cable and disappeared into the backstage shadows.

The Joker's henchmen shoved Julie up onto the stage and forced her to walk closer to the madman with the long, thin sword. Julie was never a pushover, so Batman knew she was under the Joker's spell. Her eyes were blank and hypnotized as she shuffled to the middle of the stage.

Batman climbed out onto the lighting rig that held all the different-coloured lights above the stage.

"Ah, a beautiful lady!" said the Joker as Julie wobbled beside him, held up by masked goons holding each of her arms. "We must give the audience what it wants!"

Even mesmerized, Julie must have realized she was in terrible danger. Tears trickled down her cheeks although otherwise she appeared completely calm.

The Joker's grin grew wider as he saw her despair. "See what I mean about the miserable power in the universe that connects all things?" he asked the audience. "As long as I can share my cheerful misery with you awful people, then I know I have fulfilled my purpose of existence."

He stared out at the audience members, many of whom had tears streaming down their frozen faces. The Joker cackled to himself in delight.

"But true joy," the Joker continued, "is not simply connecting the horrors of life. The real, delicious pleasure comes from *risk*." He held up his gleaming sword and turned to face Julie. "Ready or not," he said with a grin. "Here it comes."

Batman dropped from the lighting rig, landing with his cape outstretched between the Joker and Julie. He instantly high-kicked upwards, slamming the heel of his boot against the base of the Joker's sword. **CRACK!** The blade snapped off and clattered onto the stage.

"My beautiful sword!" the Joker cried. He blinked away disappointment. Then he raised his head and grinned at Batman. "Batman," he said. "It's always such a pleasure when you drop by. Now this show is really getting good!"

The Joker stepped away from Batman as his two henchmen ran onstage with baseball bats.

Batman corrected his first assessment: one henchman and one henchwoman. It was hard to tell the difference in their baggy jumpsuits and clown masks. He stood protectively in front of Julie.

The male goon reached Batman first, holding his baseball bat over his head like he was wielding a sledgehammer. Batman easily sidestepped the henchman's clumsy attack. Batman pivoted and swung out his leg, sweeping the goon off his feet. The henchman toppled backwards, hitting his head on the stage floorboards, knocking him out cold.

Batman clapped his hands beside Julie's ears. **CLAP! CLAP!** "Run away," he ordered her. "Hide backstage."

Immediately, Julie clattered on her heels away from the fight, past Mayor Grange trapped in the tank. She slipped through the opening in the middle of the curtain.

Meanwhile, the Joker's henchwoman hung back a little, tightly holding her baseball bat up in front of her face, warily watching Batman's every move.

Batman jumped towards her, swirling his cape to his left to catch her attention. *SWISH!* When her eyes shifted to follow his cape, he jammed the base of his palm forward, hitting the middle of her baseball bat. *BONK!* The bat connected with her forehead, right above the edge of her clown mask. The female goon crumpled to the stage, unconscious.

Batman turned towards the Joker, glaring at his arch-enemy. "Are you all out of accomplices?" he asked.

The Joker rolled his eyes. "It's so hard to find good help these days."

"I know where you could get the help you need," said Batman. "Arkham Asylum."

"Oh, I have no plans to go back there," said the Joker. "That kind of help is no fun at all."

"You seem to be unarmed," replied Batman. "It's time I commit you back into Arkham Asylum myself." He took a step towards the Joker.

The Joker held up a tiny box. It had one big button and a flashing blue light. A remote control! The villain waggled a finger in Batman's face.

"Back up, Batman," the Joker said. "Or I'll flood the mayor's tank with a push of this button."

Batman stopped. He glanced over at the trapped mayor, where he could see a matching flashing blue light high on the water tank over her head. "Think before you act," he warned the Joker.

"What's the fun in that?" the Joker replied. "But I'd rather not jump to the finale yet. I have other tricks to show this awful audience first. So why don't you go and stand next to the tank while I keep performing for a while?"

When Batman didn't move immediately, the Joker waved the remote at him. "Go on," he said. "Back up. Shoo. Or I'll drench Mayor Marion Grange. And I'll enjoy it, too."

Batman grudgingly stepped backwards until he was standing right next to the tank. Mayor Grange banged frantically on the inside of the glass beside him.

Batman gestured for her to remain calm. He glanced up at the water tank and its trigger with the flashing blue light. It was too high to reach. He didn't know the frequency to jam the remote's signal, either.

Batman struggled to think of a way he could safely free the mayor and stop the Joker at the same time. One wrong move and the villain would dump all the water into her glass box.

The Joker applauded himself at centre stage. "Ladies and germs, my next trick will astound you all, and probably make some of you hungry! I'm going to pull a bird out of my hat. Now that's some quality magic!"

He removed the tall turban. As soon as the spinning emerald no longer faced the audience, the crowd began to shift restlessly in their seats.

"Don't get antsy," the Joker told them, as he started to dig inside the turban with his gloved hand. "Stay focused on me. I need your full attention if this illusion is going to be impressive. So concentrate, folks. Imagine the uncaring forces of the universe creating a beautiful big bird in my hat. Some of you are obviously not hating hard enough!"

The Joker reached deeper into the turban, leaning in past his elbow. "Where did I put that thing?" he said.

The Joker froze and grinned. "There it is," he said. He slowly pulled something out of the turban and held it up to the audience. "Ta-da!"

It was a big, brown, baked chicken.

The audience murmured, and a few sniffles and sobs could be heard.

"Oh, fine," the Joker said. He held the chicken in one hand and plopped the turban back on his head with his other hand. "There! Now you can all settle down again. Go back to being hypnotized. Look at the pretty spinning emerald! You are getting sleepy. You are in my power. Et cetera."

Batman didn't move a muscle as he heard Robin's voice whisper behind him through the centre parting in the curtain. "I haven't found Rachelle the assistant yet," Robin hissed. "I'm still looking! There are a lot of places to hide in all of Santoro's equipment. But Julie is safely hidden away."

The Joker tore a drumstick off the baked chicken and took a big bite, chewing noisily. "Mmm, delicious," he said.

Robin poked Batman in the back with something.

Batman reached behind to find that Robin was handing him a bundle of juggling clubs, handles first. He took them. Closer up, he could tell they were actually unlit juggling torches. Each had a thick, oily wick at one end.

"Use these to distract the Joker while I find Rachelle," whispered Robin.

Batman nodded.

"That's the trick!" the Joker said, his mouth full of conjured baked chicken. "Applaud, you ninnies!"

The audience clapped robotically.

"Not impressed?" asked the Joker. "Well, then, I guess it's time for the big finale – the soaking of your mayor!"

"Wait, Joker," called Batman. "We haven't seen you juggle yet!"

CHAPTER 4

BURNING DOWN THE HOUSE

Batman hurled the unlit torches at the Joker quickly. *ZIP! ZIP! ZIP!*

Without hesitation, the Joker caught all three in the air and juggled them effortlessly. "Of course I can juggle," he said. "What kind of jester would I be if I couldn't?" After a few seconds of keeping the unlit torches in the air, he threw them back at Batman, much harder now.

Batman caught them and whipped them back at the Joker. Both Batman and the Joker hurled the unlit torches as hard as they could, aiming for one another's heads. The juggling contest may have looked harmless, but it was really a vicious battle. The bases of the torches were heavy and could do real damage. They flew so fast they were blurred missiles in the air.

"Let's make this more fun!" cried the Joker. As the torches passed through his hands, he lit them with a lighter.

He and Batman now assaulted one another with burning batons. *FWOOSH! FWOOSH! FWOOSH!* The juggling battle had gone from dangerous to deadly. But even at that high speed, with the fiery torches, they were both so evenly matched at juggling that neither was ever going to hit the other.

The Joker let out a loud groan. "This is getting boring!" he said. "What's the worst thing I can do? Hmm ... I know, isn't it really, really bad to shout 'fire' in a crowded theatre?"

He hurled the burning torches into the curtain on stage right. They set the fabric alight in three splashes of flame. *FOOM!*

"Fire!" screamed the Joker, smiling.

Even mesmerized, the audience gasped in fear at the hungry tongues of blue and orange fire rising up the curtain on the right side of the stage.

Batman didn't hesitate: he ran at top speed across the stage towards the burning curtain. A theatre fire was incredibly dangerous. It could become an inferno in seconds.

When he reached the wings, Batman spotted a red fire bucket near the stage manager's podium right past the curtain. He grabbed it, pleased that it was more than half full of sand. But throwing the sand onto the flames only snuffed one of the three burning trails that was climbing upwards.

The fire was too big for the extinguisher on his Utility Belt. But he knew there must be an industrial fire extinguisher in plain sight.

It was hung on a red pole just a few steps inside the wings. Batman had seen the fire inspector's approval forms recently, as the theatre's renovations were completed. He knew that extinguisher was up to code!

Batman grabbed the fire extinguisher and pulled the pin. He released a jet of foam onto the curtain, chasing the burning yellow tongues. *VWOOSH!*

He used the extinguisher to defend the border between the side curtain and the main one crossing the back of the stage. If the fire spread to the main curtain, the intense heat would set off the ceiling sprinklers. But that could cause even more mayhem with the mesmerized audience and the Joker on the loose.

His first priority was to save everyone in the building. At the same time, it would also be a shame if the new renovations in the Monarch Theatre were ruined. Batman hated the idea of allowing the Joker to violate something he'd rebuilt to honour his parents' memory.

Meanwhile, glancing behind him as he sprayed the flames, Batman kept track of the audience members, who were getting unruly in the face of a fire.

"Pay attention to me!" the Joker yelled. "I am the only way you will survive this evening! Listen to my soothing voice and stare at the spinning emerald, you beautiful sheep. Enjoy the spectacle of Batman fighting fire! Will our hero successfully douse the fire, or will he fail us finally, turning all of us into baked chickens?"

Batman had only one streak of fire left to extinguish. He had to leap to reach the burning areas on top.

"Oh, Batman is getting close now," continued the Joker. "And I miss the spectacle of the flames already, don't you? Perhaps a righteous fire is the way to end this event, to truly give us a moment to remember? Maybe I'll set all of the curtains alight." He held up his gold lighter and flicked it, stepping back towards the curtain on his left.

"No more fires!" shouted Robin, dashing out of the left wing at the Joker. He was swinging his telescoping staff in front of him athletically.

"Wait!" the Joker cried, holding up his hand towards Robin. "I need to speak to you, Boy Wonder."

Robin stopped, but kept twirling his staff. "What?" he demanded.

"You believe in mesmerism," said the Joker in an intense voice. "Don't you, Robin? You can feel the power of this spellbinding emerald spinning here on my beautiful turban?"

Robin gulped. "Your mind tricks aren't going to work on me," he said. "I'm trained in many psychological mind-shielding techniques."

"Impressive," said the Joker. "As you stare at the deep green depths of my spinning, glimmering emerald, I am in awe of the mighty powers of your mind. But I have one simple but crucial question for you: all this training you received, was that before or after you knew you were a chicken?"

Robin blinked. Then he dropped down into a squat, waddled and began clucking.

"You've been a marvellous volunteer," said the Joker.

The Joker's female goon, who Batman had hit with the bat, climbed to her feet. She rubbed a bump on her forehead.

"You there," the Joker called to her. "Get me some strait-jackets!"

The henchwoman ran backstage and quickly returned with two strait-jackets.

Batman pulled down the smouldering remains of the right curtain and sprayed the whole thing with the fire extinguisher.

The henchwoman and the Joker forced the strait-jacket onto Robin's arms. Then they trussed him up tight in the backwards jacket. Robin clucked and peeped in panic.

The henchwoman had just buckled Robin in securely when Batman's fist bonked the top of her head. Her eyes rolled back and she dropped into a heap.

CLAP! CLAP! Batman smacked his hands together sharply next to Robin's ear. "Distract the Joker," he ordered.

Robin stood up to attention, surprised to find himself in a strait-jacket. "Was I a chicken?" Then his brain cleared and he stomped hard on the Joker's foot. *CRUNCH!*

"Ouch!" the Joker screeched. "That was entirely uncalled for. I really don't like you, Robin." He hopped up and down, and pulled out the remote control, pointing it at the tank while holding it in both hands. "The mayor gets drenched!"

Before he could press the button, Batman knocked it out of his hand as he slid the strait-jacket onto the Joker's outstretched arms. Overpowering the wiry villain, Batman swung the Joker around and crossed his arms, securing the straps behind him.

The Joker laughed. He dived forward, wrenching himself out of Batman's grip. He toppled onto his face ... and pushed the button on the remote with his nose. *BEEP!*

The water tank on top of the mayor's imprisoning glass cabinet glugged loudly as a big bubble erupted inside it.

SPLOOSH! Water gushed down onto the mayor, quickly filling the cabinet.

Mayor Grange screamed inside the box, unheard through the thick glass. The water level climbed up her body, past her neck, above her desperately raised chin and covered her head.

CHAPTER 5

THE TRICK OF THE TANK

"No!" Batman yelled. He rushed over to the tank, where Mayor Grange was thrashing in the water inside, smacking her hands against the insides of the thick, reinforced glass walls.

Batman didn't know how to get her out. He pushed his shoulder against the cabinet, but it was too heavy to topple. Was there any possible way he could break this glass?

"Batman," a voice whispered. "Back here."

He peeked around the edge of the tank. Santoro's assistant, Rachelle, stuck her face through an opening in the middle of the curtain from backstage.

"Robin found me," explained Rachelle. "He told me to wait here in safety until you needed me!"

"I need you now," said Batman. "The mayor will drown if we don't help her. How can I get her out?"

"The back panel of the tank expands like an accordion," replied Rachelle. "All she has to do is push backwards hard."

Batman looked up at Mayor Grange. She was gaping at him through the side of the tank, her eyes full of terror and panic.

"Push against the back of the tank!"
Batman yelled.

As he heard Batman's shout, the Joker
raised his head. "No, Batman!" he yelled.
"We magicians never reveal our tricks!"
He began to inch towards the tank in his
strait-jacket. "Keep your big mouth shut!"

Still trussed in a strait-jacket, too, Robin
crawled in front of the Joker, trying to head
him off.

The Joker kicked at Robin, who kicked
back. They smacked shoes and boots
together, aiming at one another's ankles.

"Mayor!" Batman shouted again. "Push
backwards against the rear panel!"

"Get out of my way!" the Joker seethed at
Robin. He growled at being blocked. As he
couldn't get past, he sat up.

Robin wobbled upright, too, just as the Joker smacked his shoulder into Robin's. They struggled up onto their knees and faced off, bumping their chests like fighting walruses.

When the Joker lunged to bite Robin's face, Robin toppled backwards and rolled away.

"Maniac!" Robin snapped.

"Sidekick," the Joker sniped back.

At the tank, Mayor Grange shook her head at Batman, bubbles streaming out of her nose. No sounds made it through the thick glass, so she couldn't hear his shouted instructions.

Batman waved his hand for her attention. He stood at an angle to her, showing that he wanted her to stand against the back of the tank. Then he pantomimed pushing backwards, overdoing his actions so she would understand.

The mayor nodded. She faced forward and slammed her back against the rear panel of the tank. *KA·CHUNK!*

As Rachelle promised, the panel expanded backwards with the mayor. At the same time, a clear glass pane slid down from the top, sealing off the tank from the new space in the expansion area. The water around the mayor drained into the tank's base.

She gasped for breath, filling her lungs with air, although to the audience in front of her, it looked like she was still underwater in the tank.

Rachelle opened the rear compartment, and the mayor tumbled backwards. Batman caught her and placed her down safely.

"Don't bother ... with me," the mayor panted. "I'm fine! Go and catch the Joker and stop him before he really hurts someone."

"I'm getting you offstage first," Batman said. He hooked his gloves under the mayor's arms and pulled her backwards through the curtain opening. Rachelle waited for them backstage and helped Batman settle the mayor down on a pile of sandbags.

"Are you sure you're unhurt, Mayor Grange?" asked Batman.

"Yes, yes," the mayor insisted. "Only my pride is damaged."

"I'll watch her until the paramedics can get to us," promised Rachelle.

Batman heard soft footsteps behind him. He turned around just in time to see a henchman swinging a baseball bat. Batman easily ducked the strike, then he rolled left to lead the goon away from Mayor Grange and Rachelle.

Batman thought they'd subdued all the henchmen. This goon must have been the one controlling the lights in the booth upstairs.

"Watch out!" cried Rachelle as the goon swung his bat again.

CLANG! The bat struck the floor in the empty space where Batman had been a second previously. Now Batman stood near the henchman, a step out of range of the bat, watching his next move carefully.

"The Joker's going to pay me extra to finish you off," the goon said gleefully.

"Good luck collecting that bonus," replied Batman. He reached out with lightning-fast reflexes and pulled the henchman's plastic mask a little to the side, sliding it off-centre. Now the goon couldn't see.

The henchman dropped his bat to claw at the mask, trying to remove it or get it back on straight.

Batman picked up the goon's wooden weapon. "Nice," he said. "You know, I'm a big fan of bats."

As the henchman straightened his mask, Batman swung the bat towards the back of the crook's legs. He pulled up as he felt the bat connect, sweeping the goon completely off his feet. *WHOOSH!* The henchman flipped backwards and banged his head on a support pole, then crumpled to the backstage floor.

"Lights out for him," Batman said. He handed the bat to Rachelle, who took it with a smile.

Batman raced through the curtain and back onstage.

What he found made his eyes grow wide. The Joker's strait-jacket lay crumpled in a heap on the floorboards. The madman was loose again.

"Batman, help!" cried Robin. The Boy Wonder was trapped inside a rectangular box that looked like a coffin. Only his head and wiggling boots were visible at either end.

"I've been wearing strait-jackets for decades," crowed the Joker. "There isn't one made that can hold me for long!"

"Whatever you're planning, Joker," growled Batman, "don't do it."

"Stop him, Batman!" screamed Robin.

Batman took a step towards the Joker, and the Joker raised an oversized hand-saw with a wooden handle. The blade warbled as it wobbled in the air.

"Now for my final trick tonight!" the Joker announced. He lowered the hand-saw towards the middle of the box.

"I'm tired of your tricks," said Batman. He pulled a Batarang off his Utility Belt, and let it fly.

The Batarang hit the long teeth of the saw at the same instant it cut into the lid of the box. *THUNK!* The teeth bent as the sharp Batarang pinned them securely to the wood like a power stapler. The Joker pulled at the hand-saw, but it only wiggled and wobbled. He cursed and let go of the handle. Then the insane clown ran at Batman, screeching in fury.

Batman swirled his cape as he shifted, letting the Joker run past him. He grabbed the turban off of the villain's head and held it up to the audience.

"Wake up!" Batman yelled. "The Joker has no power over you! This hat is just a trick – it doesn't mesmerize anyone. You're just hypnotized!"

The Joker jumped for the turban, but Batman held it out of reach.

Meanwhile, members of the audience began shouting and crying and screaming as they jumped out of their seats. A group of stronger men started running towards the stage.

The Joker heard the rowdy, furious crowd and narrowed his eyes at them. "This show is so over," he said, and he launched himself at Batman's head.

Batman swirled his cape with a flourish again, sidestepping the Joker's attack, planning to push him down as he turned.

But the Joker expected Batman's familiar manoeuvre. He skidded away from Batman's push and kept running into the wings of the stage.

"Get him, Batman!" yelled Robin, wiggling his boots. "He's getting away!"

Batman sprinted after the Joker, but he was almost bowled over by the vanishing cabinet being pushed full-speed back onstage. He had to jump to the side to avoid getting flattened.

The Joker rode the cabinet to the middle of the stage. As it slowed, he waved at the audience. "At this point," he called, "I would like to remind you ... there are no refunds!"

Before Batman could catch him, the Joker pushed the rolling cabinet again, sending it careening towards the wings as he rode along.

"My big exit!" cheered the Joker. As the vanishing cabinet hit the side curtain, the Joker opened the cabinet's door and slid inside. It banged shut and then bounced open to reveal that it was completely empty.

The Joker was gone. He'd escaped.

Batman rushed over to free Robin from the sawing box. As he pulled Robin to his feet and helped him out of the strait-jacket, the audience began to applaud. In a few seconds, they were cheering wildly, giving the Dynamic Duo a standing ovation.

Unsure how to react, Batman and Robin stood awkwardly onstage.

"Take a bow," said Rachelle, walking up behind them.

"We'll bow when we've caught the Joker," said Batman.

"Take a moment and let them show you their appreciation," replied Rachelle. "Tonight you saved their lives many times."

Batman nodded. He and Robin bowed low, sweeping their capes behind them.

Then they dashed into the vanishing cabinet together.

The door swung shut and bounced open again.

Batman and Robin disappeared into the dark night in pursuit of Gotham City's most notorious criminal.

They couldn't let the Joker get away with his dirty tricks.

# THE JOKER

REAL NAME: Unknown

OCCUPATION: Professional criminal

BASE: Gotham City

HEIGHT: 1.96 m

WEIGHT: 87 kg

EYES: Green

HAIR: Green

ABILITIES: Genius-level intelligence, chemistry and engineering skills

The Clown Prince of Crime. The Ace of Knaves. Batman's most dangerous enemy is known by many names, but he answers to no one. After falling into a vat of toxic waste, this once lowly criminal was transformed into an evil madman. The chemical bath bleached his skin, dyed his hair green and peeled back his lips into a permanent grin. Since then, the Joker has only one purpose in life: to destroy Batman. In the meantime, he's happy tormenting the people of Gotham City.

- The Joker always wants the last laugh. To get it, he's devised many deadly clown tricks. He has even gone as far as faking his own death!

- Always the trickster, the Joker designs all of his weapons to look comical in order to conceal their true danger. This trickery usually gets a chuckle or two from his foes, giving the Joker an opportunity to strike first.

- The Clown Prince of Crime has spent more time in Arkham Asylum than any Gotham City criminal. But that doesn't mean he's comfortable behind bars. He has also escaped more times than anyone.

- While at Arkham, the Joker met Dr Harleen Quinzel. She fell madly in love and aided the crazy clown in his many escapes. Soon, she turned to a life of crime herself, as the evil jester Harley Quinn.

BIOGRAPHIES

J. E. Bright is the author of many novels, novelizations and novelty books for children and young adults. He lives in a sunny apartment in the Washington Heights neighbourhood of Manhattan, New York, with his difficult but soft female cat, Mabel, and his sweet male cat, Bernard. Find out more about J. E. Bright on his website.

Luciano Vecchio was born in 1982 and currently lives in Buenos Aires, Argentina. With experience in illustration, animation and comics, his works have been published in the US, Spain, UK, France and Argentina. His credits include *Ben 10* (DC Comics), *Cruel Thing* (Norma), *Unseen Tribe* (Zuda Comics) and *Sentinels* (Drumfish Productions).

GLOSSARY

benefactor someone who gives a gift of money or support

hypnotize put another person in a sleep-like state

illusion something that appears to be real but isn't

memorial something that is built or done to help people remember a person or event

mesmerism hypnosis that involves the idea that an invisible force, called animal magnetism, exists between animals

pantomime telling of a story with gestures, body movements and facial expressions rather than words

psychological relating to the mind

renovation restoration of something that has been neglected back into good condition

scabbard case that holds a sword, dagger or bayonet when it is not in use

strait-jacket garment made of strong material designed to bind the arms of a violent or disoriented person

DISCUSSION QUESTIONS

1. Bruce and Tim decide to help the Magnificent Santoro escape from the bull before capturing the Joker in the theatre. Should they have stayed to deal with the Joker first? Should they have split up to handle both threats at the same time? Explain your answers.

2. Apart from body movements, what other ways could Batman have communicated with Mayor Grange in the soundproof Water Torture Cell? Which method do you think would have been the most effective?

3. The Joker uses hypnotism to control the crowd in the theatre. Have you ever seen someone get hypnotized? How do you think it works? Explain your answers.

WRITING PROMPTS

1. Describe the most amazing illusion or escape you've seen a magician perform. Explain how you think the trick was performed.

2. At the end of the story, Batman and Robin disappear in the vanishing cabinet to pursue the Joker. Write what happens next and describe how the Dynamic Duo captures the Clown Prince of Crime.

3. Batman and the Joker duel with flaming juggling torches. Create a super hero who uses juggling to conquer crime. Write a short story featuring your new super hero, then draw a picture of him or her.